I Am Loved

Published by Inhabit Media Inc.
www.inhabitmedia.com

Inhabit Media Inc. (Iqaluit) P.O. Box 11125, Iqaluit, Nunavut, XOA 1HO
(Toronto) 191 Eglinton Avenue East, Suite 310, Toronto, Ontario, M4P 1K1

Editors: Neil Christopher and Grace Shaw
Art directors: Danny Christopher and Astrid Arijanto

We acknowledge the support of the Canada Council for the Arts for our publishing program.

This project was made possible in part by the Government of Canada.

ISBN: 978-1-77227-281-9

Printed in Canada.

Library and Archives Canada Cataloguing in Publication

Title: I am loved / by Mary and Kevin Qamaniq-Mason ; illustrated by Hwei Lim.
Names: Qamaniq-Mason, Mary, 1985- author. | Qamaniq-Mason, Kevin, 1982- author. | Lim, Hwei, 1980-
    illustrator.
Identifiers: Canadiana 20200242873 | ISBN 9781772272819 (softcover)
Classification: LCC PS8633.A43 I26 2020 | DDC jC813/.6—dc23

Canada Council   Conseil des Arts
for the Arts   du Canada

I Am Loved

by **Mary and Kevin Qamaniq-Mason**

illustrated by **Hwei Lim**

Unnukkut! Good evening! My name is Pakak. These are my new pyjamas! This is my new bedroom in my new house.

I live here with my foster family.

At first, I wasn't so sure about living with a new family. I didn't know the kids that I was going to live with.

My bed felt strange. It felt like someone else's bed.

The house smelled different, too. My foster parents made food I had never tried before.

But most of it was actually pretty good! It turns out that I like a lot of things about living here.

Today was so fun! I went out sledding with my foster sister and we played on the big snow pile. Then we had Chinese food for dinner—it's my very favourite. I felt so happy all day.

But sometimes I feel very sad. After the fun day we had, I was so tired. When I got into bed, I looked at a picture of my *anaana*, my mom.

I started to wonder if she had a good day like I did. I wondered if she was happy. I miss her a lot.

I wish I could know what's going to happen next. When I don't know what will happen, I feel scared and angry.

Then I felt so angry, I put Anaana's picture under my bed.

I know that my anaana loves me more than anything else in the whole universe! Even though she loves me that much, sometimes she can't take care of me. That's not my fault.

It's not her fault, either. She is doing the best she can to get healthy in her body and her mind and her heart. If she gets healthy enough to take care of me, then maybe I can live with her again.

If she can't keep me safe, then I will live with someone who can.

Sometimes I feel alone.

Then I remember a secret that my *anaanattiaq*, my grandmother, told me once. I haven't seen her in a whole year and I miss her a lot. But I can still hear her whispering into my ear. Do you want to hear the secret?

Okay. Come close, and I'll whisper it into your ear . . .

Naglingniq qaikautigijunnaqtuq maannakautigi! Love can travel anywhere in an instant!

It's true! Even if I am so far away that I would have to fly in an airplane to see her, my anaanattiaq's love travels all the way to me. It travels to me in an instant every time she thinks about me (and I know she thinks about me a lot)!

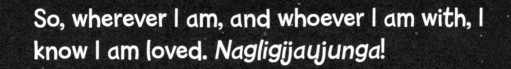

So, wherever I am, and whoever I am with, I know I am loved. *Nagligijaujunga!*

Nunarjuaq, the Land, loves me. When I walk to school and my *kamiik*, my boots, touch the ground, I can feel Nunarjuaq holding me up and giving me strength.

Siqiniq, the Sun, loves me. When I'm not sure what's going to happen to me next, I close my eyes and turn my face up to Siqiniq. I know I am safe and protected when I feel Siqiniq shining all around me.

Taqqiq, the Moon, loves me. Sometimes when I am in bed at night and I feel alone, Taqqiq sends beams of light to me. Then I know that I am not alone.

I have a huge family that loves me. I have my parents, my grandparents, my great-grandparents, my great-*great*-grandparents, and all our ancestors who lived even before *them*! I have my aunties and uncles, my brothers and sisters, and my cousins.

Even if I don't see them very much, they are still my family.

Some of my family lives in the North. Some of them live in the south. Some live in small communities. Some live in big cities.

Some of them have died, like my *amauq*, my great-grandmother, and now they are in the spirit world.

No matter how far away my family members are from me tonight, their love travels all the way to me.

None of them have ever forgotten me, and none of them ever will.

When I feel their love reach me, it's like a happy secret in my heart. I send love back to them. Even when we can't see or hear each other, I know that my heart is talking to their hearts.

I know I am loved. And so are you!

Glossary

Notes on Inuktitut Pronunciation

There are some sounds in Inuktitut that may be unfamiliar to English speakers. The pronunciations below convey those sounds in the following ways:

- A double vowel (e.g., aa, ee) lengthens the vowel sound.
- Capitalized letters denote the emphasis for each word.
- q is a "uvular" sound, a sound that comes from the very back of the throat. This is distinct from the sound for k, which is the same as a typical English "k" sound (known as a "velar" sound).

For additional Inuktitut-language resources, please visit inhabitmedia.com/inuitnipingit.

Term	Pronunciation	Meaning
amauq	a-MAUQ	great-grandmother
anaana	a-NAA-na	mother
anaanattiaq	a-NAA-nat-tiaq	grandmother
kamiik	ka-MEEK	two skin boots
Nagligijaujunga!	NAG-li-gi-JAU-ju-nga	I am loved!
Naglingniq qaikautigijunnaqtuq maannakautigi!	NAG-ling-niq QAI-kau-ti-gi-jun-naq-tuq MAAN-na-KAU-ti-gi	Love can travel anywhere in an instant!
Nunarjuaq	nu-NAR-juaq	the Land (more commonly, the Earth)
Siqiniq	si-QI-niq	the Sun
Taqqiq	TAQ-qiq	the Moon
Unnukkut!	un-NUK-kut!	Good evening!

Contributors

Mary and Kevin Qamaniq-Mason live in Ottawa. Kevin, who grew up in Iglulik, is a senior policy advisor at Inuit Tapiriit Kanatami. Mary holds a PhD in Education with a special interest in well-being and connection. They have a son and a daughter by custom adoption and are foster parents to more.

Hwei Lim draws comics (the *Boris & Lalage* series; *Spera: Volume 1*; and *Mirror*, with Emma Rios) and illustrates books (*The Spirit of the Sea* and *Dragonhearted*). Hwei lives in Malaysia.

INHABIT
Iqaluit • Toronto